HODGE PODGE LODGE

(a rubbish story)

Priscilla Lamont

The Pigwigs live happily here in Hodge Podge Lodge.
It's a bit higgledy-piggledy, as you can see.

Here are the higgledy-piggledy Pigwigs.
This is Pa Pigwig, who likes to send off for all sorts of (useful) things.

This is Ma Pigwig bringing home her shopping in lots of
bags and boxes. And just now all her lovely homemade
jams are piled up all over the place too!

This is Master Pigwig, who spends all his pocket money on snacks and fizzy pop.

And this is Little Miss Pigwig, who just likes collecting all sorts of bits and pieces.

At Hodge Podge Lodge there are always
new things to play with,

new things to wear, new things to eat ...

useful new things ...
and not very useful things too.

One way and another there is always
string to untie and sticky tape to unstick . . .

Paper to unwrap . . .
Plastic packing to scoop out . . .

Sweets to unwrap, crisp packets and fizzy
pop bottles to empty . . .

Tops to pull off, and packets and boxes of
all shapes and sizes to open up . . .

TOO MUCH STUFF!

Then one windy morning, the Pigwigs found that all that

string and plastic and paper and packing and boxes
and mess had all quite blown away.

'Nothing like a spring clean!'
cried Ma Pigwig.

DUCK didn't agree.

Duck was swimming along when a long piece of old fishing line got wrapped around her legs.

'I'M STUCK,' said Duck.

RAT didn't agree.

Rat found some plastic packing
that looked just like meringues,
so he gobbled them up
and got a horrid stomach-ache.

'OH DRAT,' said Rat.

OWL didn't agree.

Owl flew into a big piece of wrapping paper
that was blowing around in the wind.

'TOOUUU WOUERRROO OUCH,' cried Owl,
as she crashed into a big branch.

HARE didn't agree.

Hare managed to get caught
up in lots of sticky tape.

'IT'S NOT FAIR,' said Hare.

MOUSE was pleased at first
when she found an old cardboard box.
'A wonderful home for my babies,' she squeaked.

But then it rained, and the box and Mouse and
Mouse's babies all got extremely wet.
'What a rotten house,' said Mouse.

SQUIRREL had to be rescued from inside an empty crisp packet.

DEER got an old broken toy caught up on his antlers.

And FOX, the smartest of them all,
stepped on some broken glass and had to be bandaged up.

So a meeting was called and everyone came.
'This won't do!' they all cried.
'Those Pigwigs really are a nuisance.'

(Though they really weren't the ONLY nuisances.)

So they collected every bit of rubbish and
carried them all back to Hodge Podge Lodge.

'We don't want all your old rubbish'!

the animals shouted.
'So we've brought it all back.'

'Well what a fuss,' said Pa Pigwig.
'Ooh they do look cross,' said Ma Pigwig.

Then after all the animals had left,
Little Miss Pigwig had a VERY GOOD IDEA.

For days and days she was
very busy indeed,

but at last her VERY GOOD IDEA
was quite complete.

Here are some of the clever things
that Little Miss Pigwig made:

 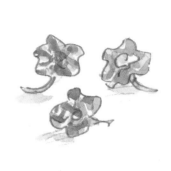 

A colourful pencil pot
from an old tin can.

Lots of pretty flowers
from the wrappers of
sweets and chocolates.

A mirror made of
painted lolly sticks and
smoothed-out silver foil.

A board game made
from bottle tops and
painted card.

A kite made from sweet wrappers, twigs,
paper and old fishing line.

Last of all she made a poster inviting
everyone to a very special event:

please
come to A
VERY SPECIAL
CRAFT
FAIR
at
Hodge Podge Lodge
ALL Welcome

SPECIAL CRAFT FAIR

At last the big day arrived and
all the animals came along.

There was something for everyone and ...
EVERYONE WAS HAPPY!

A few days later a special delivery arrived:
FOUR NICE BIG BINS.

The labels read:

"Glass bottles and jars for jam and lemonade"

"Paper and cardboard and some plastic that can be made into stuff"

And Little Miss Pigwig painted a big label for each one,
in case there was ever a muddle.

The Pigwigs are going to be more careful now
With their leftovers and bits and pieces and mess.